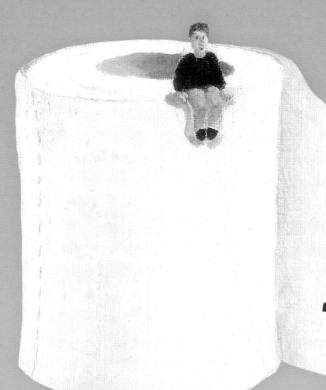

THE GIANT'S LOO ROLL

Nicholas Allan

RED FOX

A giant's toilet roll one day
Fell to the floor and flew away.

'Oh, Fe, Fi, Fo!

and Fe, Fi, Fum!

Now what shall I do to wipe my ...'

BUM - pety! Bumpety!
Bumpety - Bump!
It rolls down the hill
with a thumpety-thump!

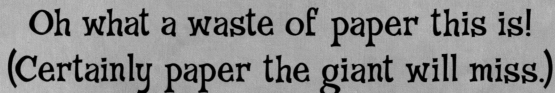

Oh what a waste of paper this is!
(Certainly paper the giant will miss.)

This rolling roll, going who knows where,
This ribbon of sheets, each ten foot square.

Rolling, rolling, flying and waving,
All this paper, so worth saving.

Rolling, rolling, waving and flying,
Look where it's going, look where it's lying.

An artist takes a single sheet . . .

And draws the toes of the giant's feet.

A class makes a dart, you can see just how.

They throw it and knock all the teachers... **KER-POW!**

A factory boss
finds a sheet
or two . . .

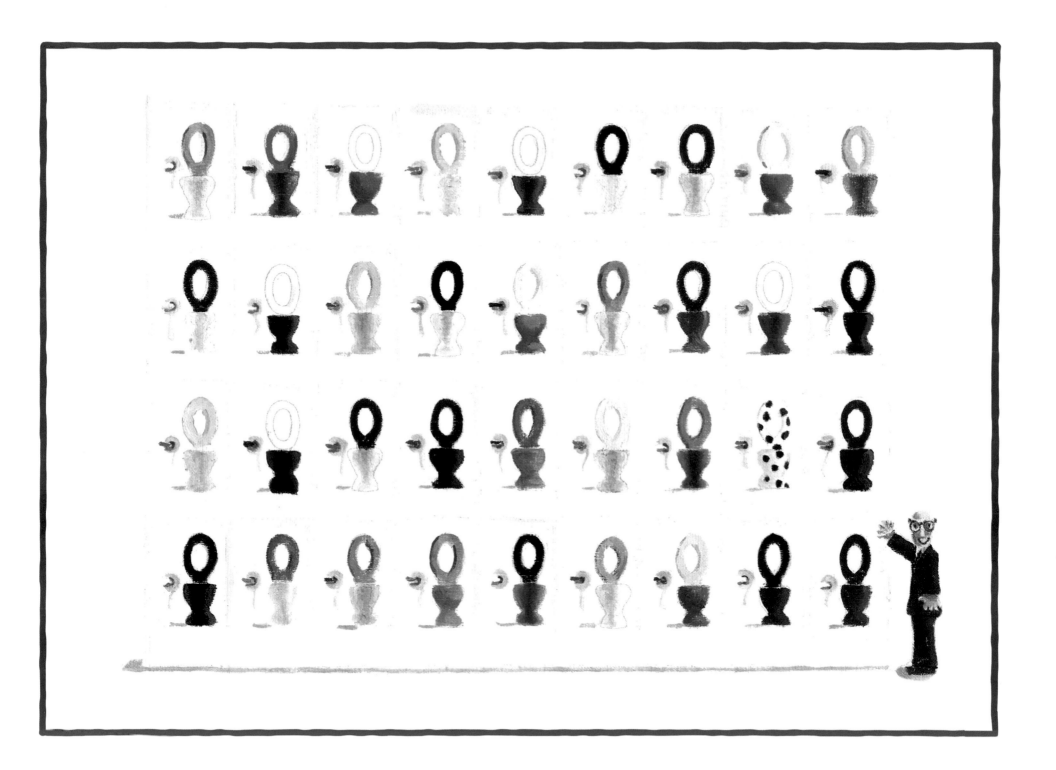

And makes paper rolls for all these loos!

Rolling, rolling, flying and waving,
All this paper, so worth saving.

Rolling, rolling, waving and flying,
Look where it's going, look where it's lying.

A tailor finds one, and with thanks . . .

She fills her shop with paper pants.

Mums and dads and children find
Some sheets for a party they have in mind.

They make party things like plates and hats
(All they need - except the snacks!).

And now the roll, it lies quite still,
It won't go on – it's run out of hill.

And the people who used all that paper for fun,
They've followed the roll to where it has come.

'There's still paper left, despite all the loss,
And it's worth giving back,' says the factory boss.

'We must thank the giant and return the roll too,
He might, by now, be in need of a poo.'

They march through the town and right up the hill
To the giant's house, by the old paper mill.

'Come on,' they say, 'just a few steps more.'
And then they arrive at the giant's front door.

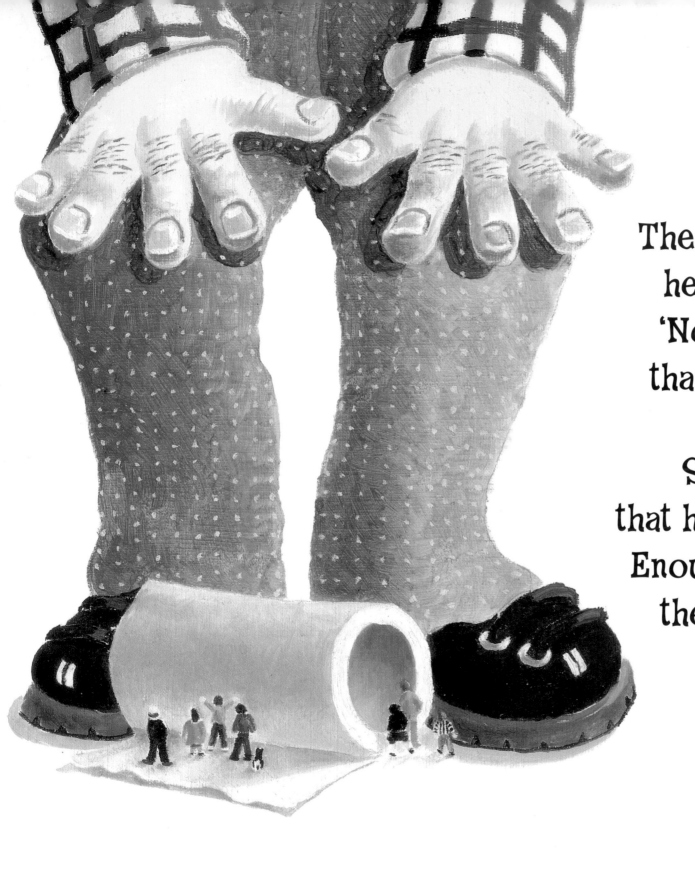

The giant is **pleased**,
he slaps his knees.
'Now I can do more
than just have a pee!'

So pleased is he
that he gives them all tea,
Enough tea, as you see,
they all need a wee!

They take it in turns in the giant's huge bowl
And then give the giant his toilet roll.

'Oh thank you!' he says, then closes the door,
And there's just enough paper . . .

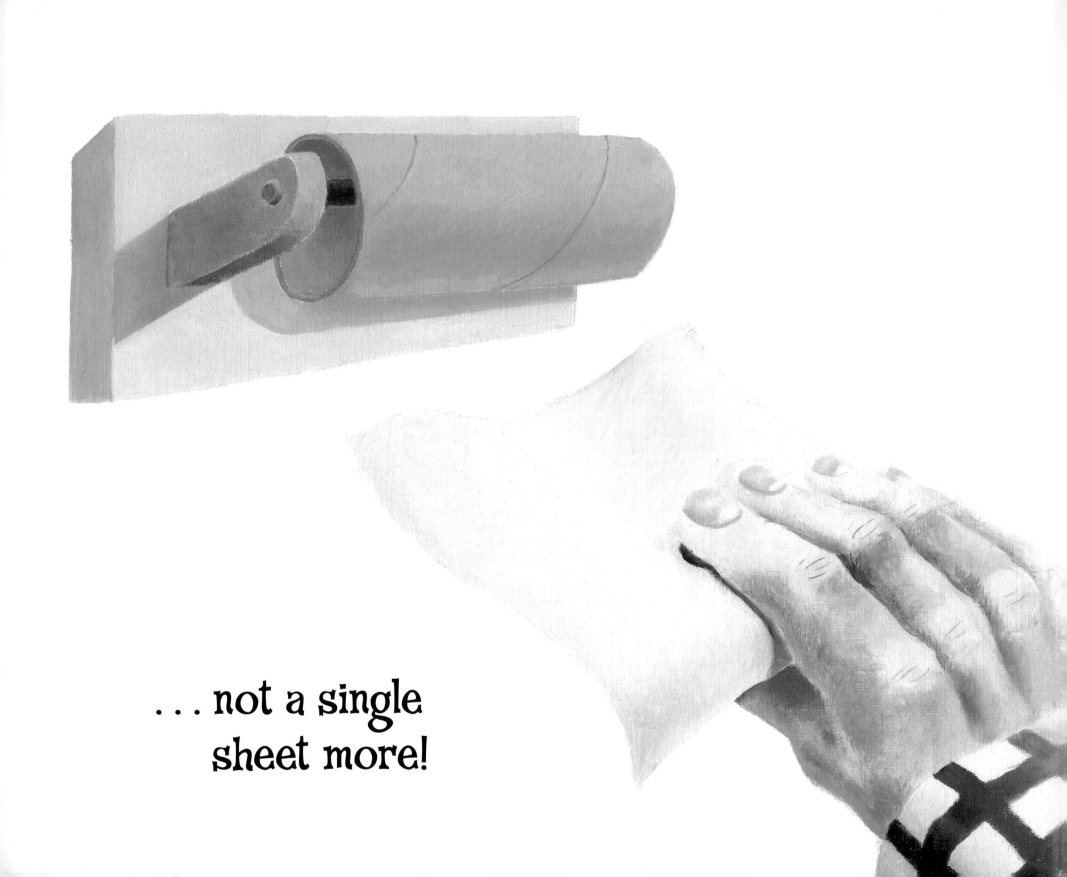

... not a single
sheet more!

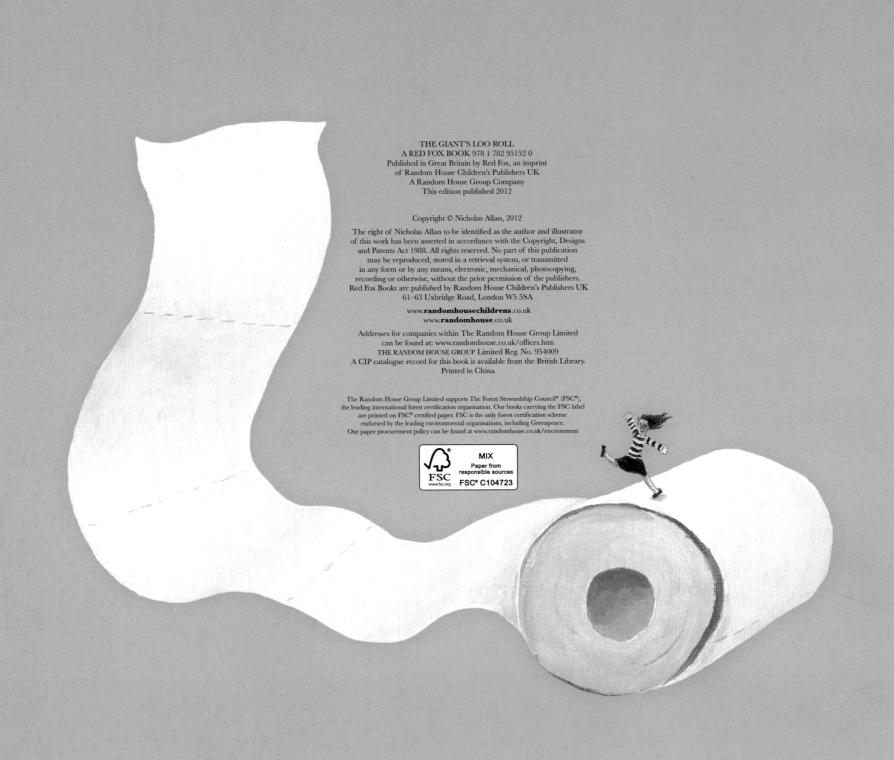

THE GIANT'S LOO ROLL
A RED FOX BOOK 978 1 782 95152 0
Published in Great Britain by Red Fox, an imprint
of Random House Children's Publishers UK
A Random House Group Company
This edition published 2012

Red Fox Books are published by Random House Children's Publishers UK
61–63 Uxbridge Road, London W5 5SA

www.**randomhousechildrens**.co.uk
www.**randomhouse**.co.uk

Addresses for companies within The Random House Group Limited
can be found at: www.randomhouse.co.uk/offices.htm
THE RANDOM HOUSE GROUP Limited Reg. No. 954009
A CIP catalogue record for this book is available from the British Library.
Printed in China

The Random House Group Limited supports The Forest Stewardship Council® (FSC®),
the leading international forest certification organisation. Our books carrying the FSC label
are printed on FSC® certified paper. FSC is the only forest certification scheme
endorsed by the leading environmental organisations, including Greenpeace.
Our paper procurement policy can be found at www.randomhouse.co.uk/environment

MIX
Paper from
responsible sources
FSC® C104723
FSC
www.fsc.org